Santa on the Loose!

By Bruce Hale

Illustrations by Dave Garbot

HARPER FESTIVAL
An Imprint of HarperCollinsPublishers

All the North Pole is in a tizzy! Someone stole Santa's toys, and it's almost Christmas Eve! Mr. Claus is in hot pursuit—can you figure out who did it?

The Suspects...

Loki the Reindeer

Emo the Elf

Softy the Snowman

Roz the Bear

Find the clues hidden on each page and help Santa catch the toy thief. You'd better hurry, though—Christmas is coming. Time is running out!

Kendra, Santa's Helper

Arlo the Penguin

Santa has just spotted something that belongs to the toy robber.
Here's your first clue—find Kris Kringle and see what he's holding.

Everyone searches high and low in the toy workshop. Santa notices something suspicious that the thief left behind. What is it?

At Ye Olde Elf Inn, Santa Claus sees something odd.
Where is he, and what's he holding?

Something is fishy at the big ice cave—and it's not just the polar bears' lunch! Locate Santa to find another clue.

As Santa Claus searches the stables, he finds something the thief must have dropped. Can you spot Santa and his clue?

Outside Kringle Manor, Santa discovers strange footprints in the snow. Find Santa to check out the footprints that the toy robber left behind.

Mr. Ho-ho-ho followed the footprints to the North Pole Mall, and it looks like he found another clue. Do you see what Santa's sniffed out?

Next, Santa noses around the hockey rink, and he spots something suspicious. Find Kris Kringle, and you'll see it too!

Santa Claus is getting warmer—and not just because he's in the ski lodge. He's found something! Now can you find *him*?

Sweet! Santa has spotted another clue at the candy factory. Locate Santa and learn the scoop.

In the Wrapping Barn, Santa spies one last sign, and it's a doozy! Find him and see if you can wrap up this investigation.

The Evidence...

Sunglasses

Wristwatch

Half-eaten Candy Cane

Torn Wrapping Paper

Hot Cocoa

Spotted Ribbon

Have you figured out who took the Christmas toys? Let's look at all the clues again.

Snowshoe
Print

Red Scarf

Green
Mitten

Black
Button

Knit
Cap

That's right! It was Emo the Elf!
He's the security chief at Santa's Workshop, and he wanted to test how quickly a thief would be caught. Emo seems pleased. But Santa's not laughing.